CULTURE IN ACTION

Song and Dance

A Journey Through Musical Theater

Elizabeth Raum

Chicago, Illinois

www.heinemannraintree.com
Visit our website to find out more information about Heinemann-Raintree books.

To order:
☎ Phone 888-454-2279
💻 Visit www.heinemannraintree.com to browse our catalog and order online.

©2011 Raintree
an imprint of Capstone Global Library, LLC
Chicago, Illinois

All rights reserved. No part of this publication may be reproduced or transmitted in any form or by any means, electronic or mechanical, including photocopying, recording, taping, or any information storage and retrieval system, without permission in writing from the publisher.

Edited by Louise Galpine, Megan Cotugno, and Abby Colich
Designed by Ryan Frieson
Original illustrations ©Capstone Global Library, Ltd.
Illustrated by Cavedweller Studio, Randy Schirz
Picture research by Liz Alexander
Originated by Capstone Global Library, Ltd.
Printed and bound in China by China Translation & Printing Services, Ltd.

14 13 12 11 10
10 9 8 7 6 5 4 3 2 1

Library of Congress Cataloging-in-Publication Data
Raum, Elizabeth.
  Song and dance : a journey through musical theater / Elizabeth Raum.
       p. cm. -- (Culture in action)
  Includes bibliographical references and index.
  ISBN 978-1-4109-3921-0 (hc)
 1. Musicals--History and criticism--Juvenile literature. I. Title.
  ML2054.R38 2011
  792.609--dc22
                                    2009051119

Acknowledgments

The author and publishers are grateful to the following for permission to reproduce copyright material:

We would like to thank the following for permission to reproduce photographs: Alamy p. **26** (© David Anthony); Corbis pp. **6**, **12** (© Bettmann), **22** (© Jonathan Drake/Reuters), **23** (© Julian Martin/epa); Getty Images pp. **5** (Peter Kramer), **8** (Popperfoto), **9** (Eileen Darby/Time & Life Pictures), **10** (Hulton Archive), **14** (AFP), **15** (Sean Gallup), **16** (Fred R. Conrad/New York Times Co.) **19** (AFP), **20** (AFP), **24** (Dan Kitwood); The Kobal Collection pp. **4**, **11** (MGM); Rex Features pp. **7** (Alastair Muir), **13**, **18** (ITV), **27** (© Disney/Everett).

Cover photograph of *Billy Elliot* the Musical reproduced with permission of Press Association Images (Yui Mok/PA Wire).

We would like to thank Ken Cerniglia and Jackie Murphy for their invaluable help in the preparation of this book.

Every effort has been made to contact copyright holders of any material reproduced in this book. Any omissions will be rectified in subsequent printings if notice is given to the publisher.

All the Internet addresses (URLs) given in this book were valid at the time of going to press. However, due to the dynamic nature of the Internet, some addresses may have changed, or sites may have changed or ceased to exist since publication. While the author and Publishers regret any inconvenience this may cause readers, no responsibility for any such changes can be accepted by either the author or the Publishers.

Author
When she's not writing books for young readers, Elizabeth Raum enjoys going to see plays and movies. Her favorite musicals are *Singing in the Rain* and *The Wizard of Oz*.

Literacy consultant
Jackie Murphy is Director of Arts at the Center of Teaching and Learning, Northeastern Illinois University. She works with teachers, artists, and school leaders internationally.

Expert
Ken Cerniglia is a writer and director with a Ph.D. in theater history. As dramaturge and literary manager for Disney Theatrical Group, he also develops musicals for schools, community theaters, and Broadway.

Contents

Story, Song, and Dance 4

The Early Days of Musicals 6

The Golden Age of Musicals 8

Creating Spectacles 14

The Sources 18

Musicals Everywhere 22

Performing in Musicals 24

One Hundred Years of Musicals 28

Glossary 30

Find Out More 31

Index 32

Some words are printed in bold, **like this**. You can find out what they mean by looking in the glossary on page 30.

Story, Song, and Dance

Have you ever gone to see a musical at your local high school or theater? Perhaps you have seen a movie musical such as *Beauty and the Beast* (1991), *The Sound of Music* (1965), or *The Wizard of Oz* (1939). The first musicals were stage shows. Later, movie musicals became popular, too.

Musicals are plays that use **dialogue** (spoken words), music, and **lyrics** (words to songs) to tell a story. Sometimes one person writes the entire musical. But often a **librettist** authors the story (called the **libretto**, or book), a **composer** creates the music, and a **lyricist** writes the words that are sung.

It takes many people to put on a musical. Actors, singers, dancers, and musicians perform in the show. Designers create scenery and costumes. Stage crews set up the stage, manage the lights, and keep the sound systems operating.

This 1939 poster was used to advertise the move musical *The Wizard of Oz*.

Broadway and the West End

In New York City the theater district is located around Times Square. It is called Broadway. With 40 theaters, Broadway is the largest theater district in the United States. The London theater district, called the West End, contains over 40 theaters. Most new musicals begin in either New York or London. If they are successful, they may go on national or international tours. Today, musicals are popular in many parts of the world.

Ticket holders line up outside Broadway's Majestic Theater to see a performance of *The Phantom of the Opera*. Broadway is a street that runs through New York City and gives the theater district its name.

An audience of millions

In 2007–2008, Broadway theaters sold over 10 million tickets to musicals. Another 15 million tickets were sold to shows on tour in U.S. and Canadian cities. About 13 million people attended shows in London's West End theater district.

The Early Days of Musicals

During the 1800s, variety shows with music, dance, and comedy acts became popular. In the United States, these shows were called **vaudeville**. In the United Kingdom, variety shows were held in **pubs** called music halls.

Melodramas, on the other hand, were stage plays with exciting stories and **stereotyped** (exaggerated) characters such as a handsome hero, a beautiful heroine, or a robber in a black hat. Music helped create excitement, fear, or humor.

In 1866 a melodrama called *The Black Crook* was rehearsing in William Wheately's New York theater. Wheately thought the show was dull, so he hired a troop of 100 French ballerinas to dance during the boring parts. The audience enjoyed the mix of melodrama and dance so much that the show played for 16 months. *The Black Crook* is often considered the first U.S. musical.

French ballerinas were used to make *The Black Crook* more interesting.

People still enjoy *H. M. S. Pinafore*. This production took place in London.

British blockbuster

In May 1878, a British **operetta** (light or comic opera), *H. M. S. Pinafore* by William Gilbert and Arthur Sullivan, opened in London. In this operetta, silly mix-ups occur when a sailor falls in love with a ship captain's daughter. The show was a huge hit in Britain. It was a success in the United States, too. Audiences loved the lively music and funny situations.

Early musicals

The success of shows like *The Black Crook* and *H. M. S. Pinafore* encouraged writers and **composers** to create more shows that combined melodrama with the singing and dancing of vaudeville. In both the United States and Britain, musical theater blossomed. Early musicals included comic plays, popular singers, and dancing girls. Often one act followed another without much connection.

The Golden Age of Musicals

In the United States, **composers** like George M. Cohan, Jerome Kern, and Irving Berlin wrote dozens of songs for Broadway musicals. At first, musicals focused on the singing, dancing, and costumes instead of the stories.

That changed in 1927, when Jerome Kern and Oscar Hammerstein II wrote *Show Boat*. For the first time in a musical, the story and music worked together to create a story. *Show Boat* takes place on a Mississippi River boat. Unlike many musicals of the day, *Show Boat* tells a sad story about the difficulties faced by a black woman married to a white man. The music included love songs, as well as **blues** and **ragtime**, two African American musical styles.

Irving Berlin

Irving Berlin (1888–1989), a Jewish Russian who came to the United States as a child, wrote the music for 19 Broadway shows and 18 movie musicals. His famous songs include "There's No Business Like Show Business," "God Bless America," and "White Christmas."

Composer Irving Berlin wrote the music for many Broadway shows and movie musicals.

A great wave of musicals followed the success of *Show Boat*. In 1927–1928 a record 264 shows played on Broadway. The years from 1927 to 1959 are considered the "golden age" of musicals.

Actress Jan Clayton dances in the 1946 **revival** of *Showboat*.

Lights and sounds

Theaters in the 1800s used gas or oil lamps. In 1881 London's Savoy Theatre became the first theater in the world to use electric lights. Today, stage designers use computers to create exciting lighting effects.

In early theaters, actors had to learn to speak loudly and clearly so the audience could hear each and every word. Today, complicated sound systems help the audience to hear the actors. They also provide special sound effects.

Movie musicals

The invention of movies with sound made movie musicals possible. In 1927 *The Jazz Singer* became the first movie musical. Audiences were amazed and delighted to hear actor Al Jolson sing.

Then in 1929 the Great Depression began. This was a period of economic hardship that lasted through the 1930s. During this time, movie musicals lifted people's spirits. Many Broadway actors and composers moved to Hollywood to make movies.

Movies allowed **special effects** that could not be accomplished in theaters. Dancers such as Fred Astaire and Gene Kelly, singers such as Judy Garland, and comedians such as Mickey Rooney starred in dozens of movie musicals during the 1930s, 1940s, and 1950s.

Busby Berkeley

U.S. director Busby Berkeley (1895–1976) created successful Hollywood movies during the 1930s and 1940s. He brought a new way of staging dance numbers to movie musicals. He arranged dancers in complicated patterns and filmed them from unusual angles.

Busby Berkeley planned complicated dance numbers like this for the 1933 movie *Footlight Parade*.

Shows about shows

Often movie musicals featured storylines about staging a show. The 1942 movie *Holiday Inn*, starring Bing Crosby and Fred Astaire, is an example. In *Holiday Inn*, a singer leaves show business to become a farmer. When he finds farm life too difficult, he decides to use the farm to put on shows during holidays. Irving Berlin (see page 8) wrote 12 songs for this movie, including "White Christmas."

Singin' in the Rain

In 1952 U.S. actor and dancer Gene Kelly codirected and starred in the movie *Singin' in the Rain*. It tells the story of silent film stars forced to make the switch to "talkies." In 2006 the American Film Institute ranked it as the best movie musical ever made.

The rain falling on gene Kelly as he sang and danced to "Singin' in the Rain" contained milk. The mix of milk and water showed up better on film than plain water, but it made Kelly's suit shrink!

Gene Kelly is shown here singing the title song *Singin' in the Rain*.

Competing with the movies

During the 1930s, people continued to go to the movies, but the Depression hurt attendance at live theaters. For example, in February 1934 there were only two musicals playing on Broadway. However, when **World War II** began in 1939, people returned to the theaters. New York and London theaters provided relief from worry about war.

Rodgers and Hammerstein years

From 1943 to 1959, Richard Rodgers and Oscar Hammerstein II ruled Broadway. Rodgers composed the music. Hammerstein wrote the **librettos** and **lyrics**. Their first show, *Oklahoma!* (1943), told a love story set in Oklahoma during the early 1900s. It included U.S. **folk** (traditional) tunes. As in the musical *Show Boat* (see page 9), the songs and dances in *Oklahoma!* helped to tell the story.

In 1951 Richard Rodgers (at the piano) and Oscar Hammerstein II (standing) worked with children who wanted to be in the musical *The King and I*.

Rodgers and Hammerstein's musicals, like this 2006 performance in London of *The Sound of Music*, remain popular.

After the success of *Oklahoma!*, Rodgers and Hammerstein wrote several more musicals. *Carousel* opened in 1945, followed by *South Pacific* (1949), and *The King and I* (1951). Audiences loved the shows. Rodgers and Hammerstein musicals were hits because the music fully blended with interesting stories.

The Sound of Music

Rodgers and Hammerstein wrote nine musicals together. In 1959 they wrote *The Sound of Music*, based on Maria von Trapp's nonfiction book about her family. The 1965 movie version, starring Julie Andrews, is one of the most popular movies ever made.

Creating Spectacles

Many different parts come together to make a great musical. This can create some amazing **spectacles**.

In the 1980s, British **composer** Andrew Lloyd Webber's musicals took over London and Broadway. In 1981 Webber wrote the music for *Cats*, a musical based on poems by T. S. Eliot. Humans dressed as cats sang and danced. The costumes were spectacular, as were the stage sets. In 1986 Webber's *Phantom of the Opera* opened in London, and later it opened throughout the world. The amazing costumes and scenery thrilled audiences. So did the music.

Special costumes and make-up turn these actors into cats for a 2005 Russian production of Andrew Lloyd Webber's *Cats*.

Andrew Lloyd Webber

British composer Andrew Lloyd Webber (b. 1948) became fascinated with musicals at a young age. He was only 20 years old when he worked with **lyricist** Tim Rice to write *Joseph and the Amazing Technicolor Dreamcoat* (1968). Later, they wrote *Jesus Christ Superstar* (1970) and *Evita* (1976). With others, he produced *Cats*, *The Phantom of the Opera*, and *Starlight Express* (see box).

Megamusicals

Webber's musicals are sometimes called **megamusicals**. Megamusicals use lighting, sound, and other **special effects** to add excitement to the show. For example, the first scene of *The Phantom of the Opera* features a huge mechanical elephant. In the third scene, the leading actress disappears into a mirror. Later, a huge ceiling light called a chandelier swings wildly before crashing to the ground. The special effects and music play on the audience's emotions.

Roller-skating musicals

Webber's *Starlight Express* (1984) was the first musical in the world performed entirely on roller skates. In July 2007, another roller-skating musical, *Xanadu*, **premiered** on Broadway.

Starlight Express was the first musical performed entirely on roller skates. The production pictured here took place in Leipzig, Germany.

Dance!

Dance also adds to the spectacle of musicals. **Choreographers** are the people who help performers tell a story through movement. They arrange the dances and work with dancers during rehearsals. Some choreographers have become writers or directors.

Early musicals used large groups of tap and ballroom dancers. Later choreographers combined dancing styles. They used ballet, modern dance, and tap in a single show. Recent musicals add rock-and-roll and **hip-hop**, too.

Jerome Robbins

U.S. choreographer Jerome Robbins (1918–1998) was a talented ballet dancer. He began his choreography career in ballets before working in musical theater and movies. Among his most famous musicals is *West Side Story*, which premiered in 1957. Robbins developed the story, based on William Shakespeare's *Romeo and Juliet*. He codirected and choreographed the musical both as a Broadway show and a movie musical.

Choreographer Jerome Robbins works with a ballerina in New York City in 1990.

MUSIC ACTIVITY

Create a musical surprise

In March 2009, people waiting for the train in Antwerp, Belgium, got a musical surprise. Two hundred men and women danced to a recording of Julie Andrews singing "Do-Re-Mi" from The *Sound of Music*. People were surprised and delighted by the unexpected show. Thousands of people have watched the video. Now it is your turn to create a musical surprise.

Steps to follow:

1. Choose a familiar tune from a musical.

2. Plan simple dance steps to go with the song as you listen to it. Then find some friends to dance with you.

3. Chose simple costumes—colored T-shirts, scarves, or baseball caps—that fit the mood of the dance.

4. Now give someone a "musical surprise!" Perform your dance in a public place, such as the school playground, a local park, your driveway, or the school cafeteria. Be sure to ask for permission first.

5. See how surprised everyone is!

Dancers often perform the same movements together. It takes lots of practice.

The Sources

Where do writers get the ideas for musicals? Some musicals—like *The Phantom of the Opera*—began as novels. *Annie* (1977) is based on a comic book. *Wicked* (2003) is based on a book by Gregory Maguire, which used characters created by L. Frank Baum in the novel *The Wonderful Wizard of Oz*.

Recently, several nonmusical movies have been turned into stage musicals. *Hairspray* (2002), *Billy Elliot* (2005), and *Legally Blonde* (2007) were movies before they became Broadway musicals.

Some musicals begin with songs. British writer Catherine Johnson wrote a simple story connecting the hit songs of the Swedish singing group ABBA. It became *Mamma Mia!* (1999). *Movin' Out* (2002) is a musical built around Billy Joel's songs.

The musical *Wicked* retells the story of *The Wizard of Oz*.

This revival of *Chicago* played in Madrid, Spain, in 2009.

Revivals

Sometimes old musicals can provide new inspiration. **Revivals** are new productions of old shows. Theaters often stage well-known shows because they attract an audience.

The musical *Chicago* **premiered** in New York in 1975. It is the story of murder during the 1920s in Chicago. The show ran for over two years. *Chicago* was **revived** on Broadway in 1996.

Longest-running show

The longest-running musical in history is *The Fantasticks*. It premiered on May 3, 1960, and closed on January 13, 2002, after 17,162 performances. It was revived in 2006.

By 2007 over 5,000 audiences had seen the show in New York, making it the longest-running revival in musical history. *Chicago* has toured the world in English-language versions, as well as in Swedish, Dutch, Russian, Italian, and French. In 2002 it was made into an award-winning movie.

Disney musicals

Walt Disney movies are also sometimes a later source for musicals. Animated movies like *Snow White and the Seven Dwarfs* (1937) were among the earliest movie musicals. They wove music and dancing into the stories, often based on fairy tales. Disney has continued to create animated musicals like *The Little Mermaid* (1989) and *Beauty and the Beast* (1991).

In 1994 Disney moved to Broadway and developed a stage musical version of *Beauty and the Beast*. Like *Phantom of the Opera*, *Beauty and the Beast* includes **special effects**. For example, the beast turns into a prince. In 1997 Disney's movie *The Lion King*, with music by Elton John, also became a stage musical. *The Lion King* uses puppets and masks to represent African animals. Most international productions of *The Lion King* are done in local languages.

A production of *The Lion King* was staged in South Africa in 2007.

ART ACTIVITY

Design an animated character

Animated movies and musicals begin with drawings. Imagine that your job is to draw one of the main characters in a new animated musical based on a story such as Jack and the Beanstalk, Little Red Riding Hood, or the Boy Who Cried Wolf.

Steps to follow:

1. Decide whether what character you will draw. Do you want the character to look traditional or modern?
2. Begin sketching. Your drawing must reveal something about the character. Can you make your character look brave, frightening, funny, or clever?
3. Draw the image on a clean sheet of paper. Add details and colors.
4. Now write a short sentence or a few words to describe your character.
5. When you are done, share your drawing with others.

It's fun to see what others have drawn and to share your own ideas.

Musicals Everywhere

Many U.S. or British musicals tour the world, drawing large audiences. But other countries also produce their own musicals—both on stage and in the movies.

One of the most successful musicals to play in New York and London comes from France. *Les Misérables*, based on a French novel about the French Revolution (1789–1799), opened in Paris in 1980. It opened in London in 1985 and is the longest-running musical in West End history. *Les Misérables* was also a hit on Broadway.

Sarafina! is a South African musical, using a story and music from Africa. It **premiered** in Johannesburg in 1987 and moved to Broadway in 1988. In 1992 *Sarafina!* became a movie.

Asia

Asian theater companies often perform U.S. and British musicals in their own languages. One theater company in Japan has been performing *The King and I* for over 35 years. Koreans enjoy U.S. and British musicals, but they are creating their own musicals, too. *The Last Empress* (1995) is an original South Korean musical.

Les Misérables is one of the most successful musicals ever. This cast is performing the show in Singapore.

Bollywood

The Indian film industry, which is called Bollywood, produces more movie musicals than any other country in the world. The movies are often **melodramas** that include lively singing and dancing. The dancing combines well-known Indian dance steps with popular western dances.

Mexican musicals

Traditionally, musicals have not been popular in Mexico. However, beginning in 2005 the musicals *Selena El Musical* ("Selena the Musical") and *Hoy No Me Puedo Levantar* ("Today I Can't Get Up") began attracting audiences in Mexico and Spain. More Mexican musicals are expected in the future.

Bollywood dancers wear bright, colorful costumes as they dance.

Performing in Musicals

Performers in musicals have studied acting, singing, and dancing. Often their first roles are in school plays or **amateur** (not professional) theater productions. Performers must try out, or **audition**, for parts by showing their talent as singers, dancers, or actors.

After auditions, rehearsals begin. At long last it is opening night. The curtain goes up, the lights go down, and the show begins.

Child performers

Today, laws require child performers to attend school or do schoolwork with a tutor at the theater or film studio. Laws also limit the hours young performs can work.

Oliver!

The musical *Oliver!* features many young performers. Based on the novel *Oliver Twist* by British author Charles Dickens, it is about a boy who escapes from an orphanage and joins a group of pickpockets. It **premiered** in 1960. In January 2009, it returned to London's West End.

These child actors performed in London's 2009 production of *Oliver!*

PERFORMANCE ACTIVITY

Be a star!

Have you ever wanted to be in a show? Here's your chance to practice being a star.

Steps to follow:

1. Watch one of the following movie musicals: *Annie* (1982), *The Sound of Music* (1965), or *Oliver!* (1968). (You can borrow a DVD from your library or rent one from a video rental store.)

2. As you watch the movie, imagine auditioning for a part in the show. Which character would you like to play? Why?

3. Learn one of the songs, line by line, and sing along with the cast.

4. Notice how the actor playing your character moves during the song. Try to perform some of the same movements as you sing.

5. Create a costume. You don't have to be fancy. A colorful shirt or scarf might be enough.

6. Now invite your friends and family to watch you perform while the DVD plays in the background.

When you're done, take a bow!

This girl practices choreography by copying the moves of the actor in the movie.

Staging your own musical

Watching musicals is fun. So is putting on your own show. You can write your own musical or you can purchase the "rights" (meaning the rights to perform it) to a well-known musical from a licensing agency. Some companies create musicals designed especially for elementary and middle schools. The price often includes not only the right to put on the show, but also the scripts and music.

Once you select a musical, you will have to hold auditions to choose the performers. A director will help the performers rehearse the show. Meanwhile, costume designers and the stage crew will work on costumes and scenery. Others will design the posters, sell tickets, and show the audience to their seats. It takes a lot of people to put on a show.

Why not give it a try?

These students perform their own version of the musical *Grease*.

Kids performing

Several recent musicals have featured young people performing. *High School Musical*, starring Zac Efron, was a 2006 Disney Channel television movie about students auditioning for a high school musical. More than 225 million viewers have watched the movie worldwide. By 2009 over 4,000 high schools, middle schools, community theaters, and professional theaters had staged their own productions of the show.

The 2009 movie *Fame* is a remake of a 1980 movie musical set in a New York City high school. It is all about teenagers who hope to become performers. *Glee* is a television series that premiered in the United States in 2009. It is about a group of high school students who hope to make the school's glee club (a singing group) a success.

In this scene from *High School Musical 2*, actors perform the song "What Time Is It."

One Hundred Years of Musicals

The following pages list major stage and movie musicals for each decade of the past century.

Decade	Stage Musicals	Movie Musicals
1900s	Ziegfeld Follies	
1920s	Show Boat	The Jazz Singer
1930s	Babes in Arms The Band Wagon On Your Toes Porgy and Bess	42nd Street Snow White and the Seven Dwarfs Top Hat The Wizard of Oz
1940s	Annie Get Your Gun Carousel Kiss Me, Kate Oklahoma! South Pacific	Easter Parade Holiday Inn On the Town Pinocchio Stormy Weather
1950s	Guys and Dolls The King and I The Music Man My Fair Lady Paint Your Wagon Peter Pan The Sound of Music West Side Story	An American in Paris Annie Get Your Gun Cinderella The King and I Oklahoma! Singin' in the Rain South Pacific White Christmas
1960s	Bye Bye Birdie Cabaret Fiddler on the Roof Hair Hello, Dolly!	Camelot Chitty Chitty Bang Bang Funny Girl The Music Man My Fair Lady

Decade	Stage Musicals	Movie Musicals
1960s cont'd	Man of La Mancha Oliver!	Oliver! The Sound of Music West Side Story
1970s	Annie A Chorus Line Chicago Evita Godspell Sweeney Todd	All That Jazz Fiddler on the Roof Grease Hair Jesus Christ Superstar Man of La Mancha
1980s	42nd Street Cats Les Misérables The Phantom of the Opera Sarafina! Starlight Express	Annie A Chorus Line Fame Footloose The Little Mermaid
1990s	Fosse The Lion King Ragtime Rent The Who's Tommy	Beauty and the Beast Evita The Lion King Selena
2000s	Billy Elliot Hairspray Legally Blonde Mary Poppins Wicked	Chicago Hairspray Moulin Rouge! Once The Phantom of the Opera

Glossary

amateur person who participates in an activity for pleasure rather than for money

audition to try out. Actors must audition for a part in a musical.

blues kind of folk music originating with African Americans that often has a sad sound

choreographer person who creates dances or plans and arranges dance movements

composer person who writes music

dialogue words in a play. The story of a musical is told through dialogue.

folk music traditional to a region

hip-hop popular type of dance and music genre. Some recent musicals include hip-hop dance numbers.

librettist person who writes the text or words to a musical

libretto text or words to a musical

lyricist person who writes the words to a song

lyrics words to a song

megamusical musical that uses startling technical effects, such as lighting, sound, and other effects

melodrama stage play with an exciting story line designed to play on the audience's emotions or feelings

operetta theatrical production like an opera but lighter and more popular in subject and style and contains spoken dialogue

premiere to have a first show

pub place that serves drink and food

ragtime style of early jazz music

revival new production of an old play. *Oliver!* became a revival.

revive to put on a show again

special effect unusual sound or sight that add to the excitement of a performance

spectacle large-scale and impressive show or display

stereotype exaggerated portrait of a person or group

vaudeville variety show with music, dance, and comedy acts following one another

World War II war from 1939–1945 in which Great Britain, France, the United States, and other Allies defeated Germany, Italy, and Japan

Find Out More

Books
Dunn, Mary R. *I Want to Be in Musicals*. New York: PowerKids, 2009.

High School Musicals series. New York: Rosen, 2009.

Schumacher, Thomas. *How Does the Show Go On? An Introduction to Theater.* New York: Disney Books, 2007.

Underwood, Deborah. *Staging a Play.* Chicago: Raintree, 2009.

Websites
Children's Creative Theater Guide
http://library.thinkquest.org/5291/
This website will teach you more about putting on your own performance.

Great Performances: Musical Theater
www.pbs.org/wnet/gperf/genre/musical_theater.html
Learn more about great musicals from this PBS website.

Place to visit
The Theater Museum
40 Worth Street Suite 824
New York, NY 10013
www.thetheatremuseum.org

Index

animated musicals 20, 21
Asia 22
auditions 24, 26

Beauty and the Beast 4, 20, 29
Berkeley, Busby 10
Berlin, Irving 8, 11
The Black Crook 6, 7
Bollywood 23
Broadway 5, 8, 9, 10, 12, 14, 15, 16, 19, 20, 22

Cats 14, 29
Chicago 19, 29
child performers 24, 27
choreographers 16
composers 4, 7, 8, 10, 12, 14
costume designers 4, 26
costumes 8, 14, 26

dance 4, 6, 7, 8, 10, 11, 12, 14, 16, 17, 20, 23, 24
dialogue 4
directors 10, 11, 16, 26
Disney movies 20, 27

Fame 27, 29
The Fantasticks 19

Gilbert, William 7
Glee 27
"golden age" 8–9
Great Depression 10, 12

Hammerstein, Oscar, II 8, 12–13
High School Musical 27
H. M. S. Pinafore 7
Holiday Inn 11, 28
Hollywood 10

India 23

The Jazz Singer 10, 28
Jolson, Al 10

Kelly, Gene 10, 11
Kern, Jerome 8
The King and I 13, 22, 28

Les Misérables 22, 29
librettos 4, 12
lighting 9, 15
The Lion King 20, 29
lyricists 4, 14
lyrics 4, 12

Mamma Mia! 18
megamusicals 15
melodramas 6, 7, 23
Mexico 23
movie musicals 4, 8, 10, 11, 13, 16, 19, 20, 22, 23, 27, 28, 29
movies 18, 20
music halls 6

Oklahoma! 12–13, 28
Oliver! 24, 25, 28

performers 4, 9, 10, 11, 16, 24, 26, 27
Phantom of the Opera 14, 15, 18, 29
rehearsals 6, 16, 24, 26
revivals 19
Rice, Tim 14
rights 26
Robbins, Jerome 16
Rodgers, Richard 12–13

Sarafina! 22, 29
Savoy Theatre 9
scenery 4, 14, 26
Show Boat 8–9, 28
Singin' in the Rain 11, 28
songs 4, 8, 11, 12, 18
The Sound of Music 4, 13, 17, 25, 28
sound systems 9, 10, 15
sources 13, 14, 16, 18, 19, 20, 22, 24
special effects 9, 10, 15, 20
stage crews 4, 26
stage designers 4, 9
Starlight Express 14, 15, 29
Sullivan, Arthur 7

ticket sales 5, 26
timeline 28–29
tours 5, 19, 20, 22

vaudeville 6, 7

Webber, Andrew Lloyd 14, 15
West End 5, 12, 14, 22, 24
West Side Story 16, 28
Wheately, William 6
World War II 12